KITTEN CROWD

Ben M. Baglio

KITTEN CROWD

Illustrated by
Paul Howard

Cover illustration by
Chris Chapman

A
LITTLE APPLE
PAPERBACK

SCHOLASTIC INC.
New York Toronto London Auckland Sydney

Special thanks to Sue Welford.
Thanks also to C. J. Hall, B.Vet. Med., M.R.C.V.S., for reviewing
the veterinary material contained in this book.

ISBN 0-590-18742-2

12 11 10 9 8 7 6 5 4 3 2   8 9/9 0 1 2/0

Printed in the U.S.A.   40
First Scholastic printing, November 1997

Contents

DOES ANYONE WANT
A FREE KITTEN?
If So,
tell Katie Greene,
Class Four
or phone Welford 706354

1

A Problem for Mandy

"What's the hurry, Mandy?" Mr. Simpson, the school janitor, called after Mandy Hope as she ran down the corridor toward the front doors.

"I've been cleaning out the gerbils' cages," Mandy said, out of breath. "And I forgot to tell James I'd be late. He'll be wondering where I am!"

James Hunter was Mandy's best friend. They always rode their bikes home together. Helping with Terry and Jerry, the class gerbils, was one of Mandy's favorite things at school. She loved animals. Being allowed to help look after the school gerbils was almost like having pets of her very own.

By the main entrance door was the school bulletin board. You could put all sorts of notices up on the bulletin board. If you wanted to sell or buy anything, that was the place to let people know.

As she passed the board, one large ad caught Mandy's eye. She stopped to see what it said.

Does anyone want a free kitten?
If so, tell Katie Greene, Class Four,
or phone Welford 706354

"That's me," a voice said behind her. "I've just put that ad up."

Mandy turned to see a girl about eight years old, a year younger than herself, staring at her.

"Are the kittens yours?" Mandy asked.

Katie nodded. "We're moving soon and Dad says we can only take their mother, Tabby, with us," she explained.

"Why?"

Katie looked sad. "He said seven cats is too many."

"Seven?" Mandy said.

"Yes, Tabby's had six babies," Katie explained.

"Oh," Mandy said. "I see. Seven cats *is* a lot."

"Would you like one?" Katie looked at Mandy hopefully.

Mandy shook her head. "I would *love* one, but both my parents are vets. They're too busy looking after other people's animals for us to have a pet of our own."

Katie sighed. "I just don't know what's going to happen if we can't find homes for them."

Mandy's heart lurched. She didn't want to think about it. Six tiny kittens with no one to love and take care of them. "Maybe I can help you," she said quickly. "I'll ask all my friends."

"Oh, would you?" Katie said.

Mandy nodded. "And my mom and dad might know someone. I'll ask as soon as I get home."

Katie's eyes shone. "Thanks."

Mandy made up her mind there and then. She would do everything she could to help Katie find homes for her kittens.

It wasn't going to be easy. Most people Mandy knew already had a pet. But she had lots of friends in the village. Surely some of them would like a kitten.

Mandy swung her bag onto her shoulder. She went through the main doors out into the playground. Katie followed.

"Would you like to come and see the kittens sometime?" she asked Mandy.

Mandy's eyes lit up. She couldn't refuse an offer like that.

"Oh, yes, please," she said. "I'd really love to."

"I live along Meadow Lane," Katie said. "Number sixteen. It's just behind the church."

"I'll ask my mom and dad if I can come this evening," Mandy said. "After dinner? Will your parents mind?"

"No, of course not." Katie shook her head.

"Could I bring my friend James?" Mandy asked. She knew James would love to see the kittens, too.

"Would he like one, do you think?" Katie asked hopefully.

Mandy shook her head. "I'm afraid he's already got a cat. And a puppy."

Katie's face fell. "Oh, I guess not. See you later." She ran on ahead to get her bike, then rode off toward the church.

Mandy was really excited. Six tiny kittens. She just couldn't wait to see them!

2

Free to a Good Home

James was waiting for Mandy by the bicycle rack. He had a worried look on his face.

James was a year younger than Mandy (he was in the same class as Katie). He and Mandy had been friends ever since Mandy had helped him choose his puppy, Blackie, from a litter of black Labradors.

"I thought you were *never* coming," James called as Mandy hurried toward him. He swung his schoolbag onto his shoulders and got on his bike.

"Race you home!" he called, pedaling off.

Mandy cycled quickly to catch up with him. "Wait," she said. "I've got something important to tell you."

They rode side by side as Mandy told James about Katie's kittens.

"Six!" James exclaimed. He took one hand off the handlebars and pushed his glasses back onto the bridge of his nose. His bike wobbled. "That's not going to be easy."

"I know," Mandy said. "But I promised to try. Will you help me, James?"

"Of course I will," James said. He loved animals almost as much as Mandy.

They cycled through the small village of Welford toward Animal Ark.

Animal Ark was the name of Dr. Adam Hope's and Dr. Emily Hope's clinic, attached to the house where they lived.

Mandy usually won the race home from school, but today she lagged behind. Her mind was still on Katie's kittens.

"Come on, slowpoke," James called.

They reached James's house and stopped outside the gate. Blackie was looking out of the front window. He always watched for James to come home, and he started barking excitedly when he saw him.

"Don't forget to ask your mom and dad about the kittens," Mandy reminded James.

"Okay," James said. "I won't." He pushed open the front gate and went through. "I'll see you after dinner."

"Yes, see you later."

Mandy waved as she pedaled quickly off toward Animal Ark.

When she got there, Mandy dumped her bike by the clinic entrance. She ran inside. Jean Knox, the receptionist, was on the telephone.

Mandy wandered around looking at the notice board. Her heart sank. Several other people had kittens for sale. That would make it even more difficult to find homes for Katie's.

On the table was a pile of pamphlets telling people how to take care of their pets. Mandy thumbed through them. Kittens, puppies, hamsters, gerbils, birds, bunnies . . . there were hints on how to look after almost every kind of pet you could think of. The Hopes believed it was important for people to know how to take good care of their animals.

As soon as Jean put down the receiver Mandy blurted out, "Can I see Mom and Dad? Are they here?"

Jean looked at Mandy over the top of her glasses. "I'm afraid your dad's gone out on a call. Your mom's here, though, if you want to see her."

Mandy rushed into the clinic. Dr. Emily was packing some medicines as Mandy came into the room. Her red hair was tied back and she wore a stethoscope around her neck. Her white vet's coat was draped across the examining table.

"Hi, Mandy," she said. "Did you have a good day at school?"

"Yes, fine, thanks," Mandy said quickly. She wanted to tell her mom about Katie's kittens. Her words seemed to tumble over themselves.

". . . And they're moving very soon so we don't have a lot of time. Oh, Mom, we've got to do something to help!"

Dr. Emily smiled gently. "Now, calm down, Mandy. This will take some thought."

She finished putting the boxes away and sat down. "Six kittens. Mandy, I don't know. It is an awful lot."

Mandy hoisted herself up on the examining table. "I know, but there must be *someone* in the village who wants them," she said. "And they *are* free."

"Yes, well," Dr. Emily said. "That will help, of course."

"And I could tell people how to look after them," Mandy added.

"Yes, I know you could," Dr. Emily said.

"James is going to ask his mom and dad," Mandy told Dr. Emily.

"Good. The more people who know, the better."

"What will happen if Katie can't find homes for them?" Mandy asked. She felt suddenly afraid. She hadn't seen the kittens yet, but she knew they would be sweet.

Dr. Emily looked glum. "I don't know, Mandy. It's not going to be an easy task, you know. Welford's small and most people already have pets of one kind or another."

"I know," Mandy said sadly. "That's the trouble."

"You could put up an ad in the waiting room, if you like," Dr. Emily said suddenly.

"Oh, Mom, can I?" Mandy's eyes shone. She jumped down. "I'll do it now."

"What will you do now?" said a voice from the doorway.

It was Dr. Adam. He came in and put his bag down on the table.

Mandy gave him a hug and quickly explained about the kittens.

"I see." Dr. Adam stroked his beard thoughtfully. "And Katie wants to find homes for them all?"

"That's right," said Dr. Emily.

"Another pet rescue, then," Dr. Adam said. His eyes twinkled as he glanced at Dr. Emily. They were both used to Mandy's schemes to help pets.

"Looks like it," Dr. Emily replied.

"I know Katie's family," Dr. Adam went on. "Mrs. Greene brought Tabby to see me a few weeks before the kittens were born. She needed some vitamin shots. I'm sure they'll be grateful for your help, Mandy."

"I know Katie will be," Mandy said. "She was so worried about the kittens, Dad. I know it's not going to be easy, but I've promised I'll do everything I can," she added. "And that's exactly what I'm going to do. Starting with that ad."

Mandy ran out to the waiting room.

"Jean, could I borrow a marker and a piece of white cardboard, please?"

"What on earth for?" Jean asked.

Mandy explained quickly.

"I see." Jean opened her drawer and took out the things Mandy needed.

Mandy sat on one of the chairs. She chewed the end of the pen and looked thoughtful. What should she write? Something that would *really* catch people's eyes. She began writing:

A WHOLE CROWD OF KITTENS
Six cute kittens
Free to a good home
Apply to
Katie Greene, 16 Meadow Lane,
or Mandy Hope at Animal Ark

Mandy handed the ad to Jean. "Would you put this up on the board, please?"

Jean got a couple of thumbtacks and went to put up the sign. She stood back to look.

"It looks great, Mandy. It does stand out. 'A

good home,'" she quoted. "Are you hoping that *one* person will take the whole"—she chuckled—"crowd?"

Mandy sighed. "It would be nice if all the kittens stayed together, wouldn't it? It's going to be bad enough losing their mother, let alone being split up from their brothers and sisters."

Jean nodded. "Yes, but I don't know who on earth is going to have enough room for six kittens."

"No," Mandy said with a sigh. "Neither do I."

3

A Box of Kittens

Mandy was so excited about seeing the kittens she could hardly eat her dinner. She sat at the table reading the class project sheet Mrs. Todd, her teacher, had given her during the last lesson.

Dr. Adam peered over Mandy's shoulder. "What's that you've got there?" he asked.

Mandy explained, "We've got to keep a journal."

"That'll be interesting," her dad said.

"Yes," Mandy said. "Then we've got to read them out loud to the class. Mrs. Todd's giving a prize for the best one."

"I'm sure you'll have a lot to put in yours," Dr. Adam said. "There's never a dull moment here!"

Mandy grinned. "That's true."

She finished her project sheet. She would have to start her journal later.

By the time Mandy had changed into her jeans it was almost seven o'clock. She hurried to James's house. She ran up the front path and knocked on the door. Blackie barked and doggie footsteps came thudding up the passageway.

James's door opened. Blackie pushed past and ran out, his tail wagging furiously as he saw Mandy. He gave a loud bark and started pulling at the laces of her shoes and making growling noises. Mandy chuckled and pushed him gently away. "Blackie!"

She bent down and hugged him tightly. "Now, Blackie!" she said more sternly. "I don't want shredded laces, thank you very much!"

She took hold of Blackie's collar. "Sit!" she commanded.

Blackie ignored her. He just barked again, then ran off around the side of the house. He stopped by the rose bed and started to dig.

James dashed after the puppy and grabbed his collar. He pulled him away from the rose bed and dragged him back indoors. He shut the door quickly before Blackie could run out again.

Mandy laughed. "You're not having much luck training him, are you?"

"No, I'm not," James said. "But I *am* trying."

"I think you've got a lot more work to do." Mandy giggled.

"Yes." James sighed. "You're right."

"Come on, then," Mandy said. "Let's go and see those kittens."

Mandy and James made their way along Main Street and across the village green.

A big man in a cap was coming the other way. It was Walter Pickard. Walter had just retired from being the village butcher. He lived in one of the tiny cottages behind the village restaurant.

Walter's face lit up when he saw Mandy and James coming toward him.

"Hello, you two." His voice was deep and kindly. "Where are you off to in such a hurry?"

Mandy told him. "You don't want another cat, I suppose, Walter?" she asked hopefully.

She knew Walter had three cats already. Maybe one more wouldn't make a difference?

Walter shook his head. "Sorry, young miss. My three young cats get into enough mischief already, thank you."

"Never mind," Mandy sighed. "I just thought I'd ask."

Walter waved as they hurried on their way. They went along the narrow footpath beside the church. It was a shortcut to Meadow Lane.

"Here we are," Mandy said as they reached number 16. She pushed open the gate. James followed her down the path.

The house looked bare and empty. There weren't any curtains on the windows. Mandy guessed they had been taken down for the move. A couple of wooden packing crates stood outside the front door. There was a pile of newspapers beside them.

Just as Mandy was about to knock, Katie came whizzing around the side of the house on her bike.

Her face lit up when she saw Mandy and James.

"Hi," she said. "I was just going to see if you were coming." She got off her bike and propped it up against the fence. "Come on, they're in the back."

Around the back of the house was a wooden shed. Katie pushed open the door.

Mandy peered in. She gave a shiver. It was damp and dark inside the shed. There were a lot of garden tools stacked up against the one wall and a lawn mower in the corner. There was only one small window to let in the light. Were the mother cat and her kittens in here?

Katie bent down and pulled aside a curtain covering the front of an old closet.

Mandy drew in her breath. There, in a cardboard box, was a small, rather thin black cat. Nestled against her side were six tiny bundles of fur.

Mandy bent down with a little cry. "Oh, look, James. Aren't they gorgeous!"

Two of the kittens were black and two were

orange. The other two were orange *and* black. They all had beautiful big eyes and tiny, screwed-up faces.

James kneeled beside Mandy. "They certainly are," he whispered.

"Does Tabby mind being stroked?" Mandy asked, looking up at Katie. She knew you had to be careful not to upset mother cats.

Katie shook her head. "No, she doesn't mind at all."

Katie kneeled down beside Mandy and James. She picked up one of the orange kittens. "Here." She gave it to Mandy. Then she picked up one of the black ones and gave it to James.

Mandy cradled the tiny creature against her chest. It mewed softly and clung to her. It had tiny, very sharp claws.

"They're so beautiful," Mandy whispered.

The sight of the six squirming, furry creatures with their tiny ears and perfect little kitten faces made Mandy's heart turn over.

Tabby gave a small meow as Mandy gently

put the kitten back. She picked up one of the black-and-orange ones and stroked it softly. She felt the tiny bones of its head and legs.

"Are you sure they're warm enough in here?" she asked Katie anxiously. She knew how important it was to keep kittens and their mothers as warm and dry as possible. She wasn't at all sure that the cats were being looked after properly.

"I kept them indoors in the closet under the stairs when they were first born," Katie explained. "But my mom has had to clear it out so we brought them out here. My mom says they're all right."

Mandy bit her lip. A damp old cardboard box was hardly all right! The kittens did look healthy enough, but she would have felt happier if they were indoors in a warm room.

"How old are they?" she asked.

"Nearly six weeks," Katie said. "Will that be old enough for them to go to new homes?"

"Just about," Mandy said. "Most kittens are

taken away from their mothers at six or seven weeks."

Katie sighed and looked sad. "I don't know what we're going to do with them. Did you ask your mom and dad?"

Mandy put the second kitten back and stood up. "Yes, they don't know anyone offhand. But I've put an ad on our board," she added. "Maybe someone will see it at the clinic tonight."

"Oh, I hope so," Katie said. "We're moving on Saturday."

"Saturday!" James exclaimed. "We'll *never* find homes by then."

Mandy frowned at him. "Yes, we will," she said firmly. "I know we will. We've got to!"

Before they went out, Mandy tucked the blanket carefully around the mother cat and her babies. She noticed that the food bowls by the box were both empty.

"She needs some milk," she said. She picked up a bowl. "And she should have fresh water to drink whenever she wants it."

"Oh, I forgot to get some," Katie said. "I had to help my mom with the packing."

"Well, can you get some now?" Mandy said. She was determined not to go home until Tabby had fresh food and water.

Mandy wanted to find homes for six *healthy* kittens, not six *hungry* ones.

Mandy and James waited while Katie went indoors to fill up the dishes.

"I don't think they're very happy in here, do you?" James said, looking worried.

"No," Mandy said, "I don't." She looked angry. "People shouldn't have pets if they can't look after them properly."

"No, they shouldn't," James agreed.

"The sooner they've got a new home, the better," Mandy added. "And it's up to us to find it for them."

"Have you asked your grandma and grandpa if they know anyone?" James asked.

Mandy shook her head. "No, but we'll drop by on the way home. Grandma knows *everyone* so maybe she'll have some ideas."

4

A Brilliant Idea

Mandy and James said good-bye to Katie at the front gate.

"I'll see you at school tomorrow," Mandy said. "Maybe we'll have some news about the kittens by then."

"I hope so," Katie said with another sigh.

Mandy and James made their way up the hill

to Lilac Cottage, where Grandma and Grandpa lived. Their car was in the driveway. Grandpa's bike was leaning up against the wall.

Grandpa was in the garden tidying up the flower beds. He grinned when he saw Mandy and James coming up the path.

"Hi, you two." He stood up and pushed his cap to the back of his head. "Grandma's baking cakes. You must have smelled them."

Mandy ran to give her grandpa a hug. "Grandma *always* just baked something," she said.

"True." Grandpa laughed. "She's gone crazy today, though. She baked enough for an army."

"Is there a village party or something?" James asked.

Grandpa shook his head. "No, they're for Westmoor House, the old folks' home. One of the residents is a hundred years old this week and they're having a party."

"Wow!" said James. His eyes were wide behind his glasses. "A hundred!"

"I bet she's baked a hundred cakes, then," Mandy said, laughing. "Let's go and see."

Grandma was in the kitchen, surrounded by trays of cakes and a mountain of dirty dishes. She gave Mandy a kiss.

"Sit down, you two," she said. "I'll just finish cleaning up, then I'll pour you both some lemonade."

"We'll help, won't we, James?" Mandy took a cloth from the rack by the stove.

"Oh, will we?" James had already sat down at the table and was gazing hungrily at the cake.

"Yes." Mandy took another cloth and put it in front of him. He got up with a sigh and started drying some of the dishes.

"Where have you been, Mandy?" Grandma asked. She dried her hands, then went over to the refrigerator. She got out a pitcher of homemade lemonade and put it on the table.

Mandy explained about the kittens. "Why don't you have one, Grandma?" she said.

"They're so sweet and it wouldn't be *any* trouble."

Grandma shook her head. "I'm sorry, Mandy. You know how we love going away on vacations and we'd hate to be tied down with a pet."

"I'd look after it if you were away," Mandy said.

Grandma shook her head again. "Sorry, Mandy. If you own a pet you have to be responsible for it yourself, not rely on other people."

Mandy sighed. Grandma was right, of course. People *did* have to be responsible for their own pets.

She dried the last of the cake tins and sat down, her chin on her hands. "You're right, Grandma. But will you ask your friends?"

Grandma gave her a hug. "Yes, of course I will. Don't look so down in the dumps. Something will turn up."

"What will turn up, Dorothy?" Grandpa came in and went to wash his hands at the sink.

"Homes," Mandy said. "Homes for kittens."

"Oh." Grandpa reached out for one of Grandma's fresh-baked cookies.

Grandma slapped his fingers. "Hands off!" she said sharply. "There won't be enough for the party."

"Spoilsport." Grandpa smiled. He looked at the clock. "I'm going to watch the football game on television. Coming, James?"

"Er . . ." James seemed reluctant although he loved football. He was still eyeing the cakes hopefully.

"Oh, here you are," Grandma said, handing him a chocolate cookie. "And help yourself to lemonade."

"Thanks, Mrs. Hope!" James said.

"Don't forget we've got to load all these into the car and take them over to Westmoor House," Grandma called as Grandpa disappeared into the front room. James followed, a glass of lemonade in one hand, his half-eaten cookie in the other.

"I won't," Grandpa called back. "Just let me know when you're ready."

Mandy still sat at the table, looking glum.

"Cheer up, Mandy," Grandma said. She began packing the cakes and cookies into tins. "How long have you got to find homes for these kittens?"

"Only a couple of days." Mandy was beginning to feel desperate. "They're moving on Saturday."

"Saturday!" Grandma put a cookie on a plate and gave it to Mandy. "We'd better get a move on then."

"Yes," Mandy said. She took a bite of the cookie. It was delicious.

"Well, I'm going to a meeting later this evening once I've delivered these goodies to Westmoor House. I'll ask everyone at the meeting, if you like."

"Thanks, Grandma, you're the best!"

Grandma peered at Mandy over the top of her glasses. "Well, we'll see about that. Don't count your chickens before they're hatched."

"Don't count your kittens, you mean," Mandy said.

When all the cakes and cookies were packed away, Mandy and James helped put them in the car.

"We could drop you off on the way, if you like," Grandpa said. "I need to drop by to see your dad anyway, Mandy. Want a ride, too, James?"

"Yes, please."

They dropped James off first. Blackie was standing with his nose through the gate.

"That puppy gets bigger every day," Grandma said, waving good-bye to James.

"And naughtier," Mandy said. "See you to-morrow," she called as James went up the path with Blackie at his heels.

When they got to Animal Ark, Dr. Emily was just going out on an emergency call.

"Dad had to go out, too," she said as she came through the gate. "I was just coming to find you, Mandy."

"She can come with us, if you like," Grandma said through the car window. "Then we'll stay with her until you get back."

"I'd be really grateful," Dr. Emily said. "Is that all right, Mandy?"

"Fine," Mandy said. She turned to her grandma. "I'll help you unload the cakes, if you like."

"That would be a great help," Grandma said.

Westmoor House was about a mile outside of the village. It was a big Victorian house that had recently been turned into a senior citizens' nursing home. There were twenty-four residents so far.

Grandpa drove up to the front door. Mandy got out and rang the bell. A woman opened the door. She was tall and slim and wore a gray suit.

The woman looked surprised to see Mandy standing on the doorstep.

"My grandma and grandpa have brought the cakes for the party," she explained.

"Oh, wonderful," the woman said. "I'm Della Skilton, the home's manager. Pleased to meet you."

Mandy helped Grandma and Grandpa take the tins to the kitchen.

"I'm so grateful," Della said. "Our residents will really appreciate it."

Mandy looked around. There was a huge stove at one end of the kitchen. She supposed there needed to be a big one when you had to be cooking for so many people every day.

Through the window, Mandy could see a long garden with lawns and flower beds. There

were two old ladies sitting in deck chairs en-
joying the warmth of the evening sunshine.

"When's the party?" Mandy asked.

"This Friday. It's going to be a big surprise
for Mrs. Brown."

"I love parties," Mandy said. "Especially surprise ones."

"Why don't you come after school?" Della
said. "You could help us hand out the food.
Everyone would love to meet you, I'm sure."

"I'd love to," Mandy said. Then she remembered the kittens. Friday was the day before

Katie moved. Mandy might still be busy searching for a home for them.

"Oh . . . but I'm sorry, I'll be really busy on Friday. I'd like to come another day, though, if I could."

Della smiled. "Come anytime, Mandy. The residents love to see young people. Some of them don't have any families, you see. And even though they all live together here, some of them feel quite lonely."

Mandy felt sad. It must be horrible not to have any family. She was lucky. She had her mom and dad and her grandparents. She had James, too, and other friends at school. Then there were James's pets, Blackie and Benji, Walter's cats, Terry and Jerry the gerbils, and all the other animals she knew. They were her friends, too.

"I'll come as soon as I can," she said. "Would that be all right, Grandma?"

Grandma smiled. "Yes, of course it would, Mandy. You could bring James, too."

"James is my best friend," Mandy told Della.

When all the cakes had been taken inside, Della went with Mandy and her grandparents to the door.

"Have a nice party," Mandy said. "Will there be lots of presents?"

"Oh, I'm sure there will," Della said.

When they arrived back at Animal Ark, Mandy's parents were still out.

"It must be almost your bedtime," Grandma said as they went in through the back door. "You run up and get ready and I'll make you a warm drink. Then I must be off to my meeting."

"Thanks, Grandma." Mandy kissed her grandma, then ran upstairs to change into her pajamas. She took her big old teddy bear off the bed and gave him a hug.

Mandy's schoolbag was on the chair. She took out her project sheet and gazed at it thoughtfully. She would have a lot to write in her journal today: finding out about the kittens; going to see them; then going to Westmoor House. She would write it before she went to sleep. Maybe tomorrow she might find homes for the kittens.

Now that really would be something to put in her journal.

Downstairs, Grandpa was watching TV. Mandy went and sat on the floor by his feet. She sipped her hot chocolate. Grandma made the best hot chocolate!

Mandy was still thinking about the kittens. She just could not get the sweet, furry creatures out of her mind.

Suddenly Grandpa gave a great laugh at the television. "Therapy dogs!" he exclaimed. "Have you ever heard of such a thing?"

"Therapy . . . what?" Mandy said.

"Therapy dogs," Grandpa repeated. "They're taking dogs into hospitals and nursing homes so that the patients can pat them."

Mandy frowned. "What do you mean?"

"Well," Grandpa said, "someone said that people feel much happier if they have pets to love and cuddle. So that's what they're doing. They're introducing good-natured dogs into places to make the residents and patients feel better."

Mandy drew in her breath. What a fantastic idea! *Everyone* knew how happy you felt if you had a pet to cuddle.

Mandy suddenly thought of the old people at Westmoor House. *They* would love to have a pet to care for.

Mandy's heart began to race. She'd just thought of something. If you could have therapy dogs, why not therapy *cats*?

She turned her face toward her grandpa, her eyes shining. "Grandpa," she said, "I've just had the most fantastic idea!"

5

Mandy's Plan

"But don't you see?" Mandy said when she had finished telling Grandpa her idea. "I bet the old residents would love to have therapy cats. They would make them feel *much* better."

"I'm sure you're right, Mandy," Grandpa said. "The cats would be great company for the residents. But *six*? Surely they wouldn't want the whole crowd?"

"There's twenty-four people there," Mandy insisted. "That's only a quarter of a cat each."

Grandpa laughed. "I can see you've been practicing your math, Mandy Hope."

"That doesn't take much working out," Mandy said.

"Why don't you ask Della?" Grandpa suggested. "There's no harm in asking. You know what your grandma always says. If you don't ask, you don't receive."

Mandy jumped to her feet. "I'll call her right now!"

Grandpa got up, too. "Not now, young lady. It's your bedtime. You'll have to do it tomorrow."

"But Grandpa!"

Grandpa shook his head. "Sorry, Mandy. It's a rule: Early to bed on school nights. One day won't make any difference. You'll get me shot if your mom comes home and you're still up and talking on the phone."

Mandy sighed. "Okay, Grandpa. I'll call to-morrow."

Upstairs, Mandy sat in bed. She tried to start writing her journal, but she only got as far as putting "Day 1." She couldn't concentrate at all. Her mind kept wandering back to the kittens. She kept seeing them in that tattered old cardboard box. She kept smelling that musty old shed. What if Della didn't think therapy cats were a good idea after all? There were only two days left. Where else could she start looking?

The next day Mandy couldn't wait for school to be over.

She had told her mom and dad about her plan at the breakfast table. Dr. Emily had looked doubtful.

"How will they cope with six kittens?" she said. "Grown-up cats are a different thing alto-gether. But six kittens could cause problems."

"There's a big garden," Mandy said. "They could play out there."

"Well," Dr. Emily said, "you'd better wait and see what Della says before you get your hopes up. But Mandy . . ." She gazed at her daughter's excited face. "Don't be too disappointed if she says no."

"I won't," Mandy said, although she knew she would be.

When it was time to go, James was waiting for Mandy by the front gate. She told him her plan as they rode their bicycles to school.

"That would be great," he said.

"We could put our pocket money together and buy them each a dish." Mandy had been making plans in her head ever since she woke up. "And I'm sure Grandpa will make them a big box if we ask him nicely."

"I'm sure my mom could find them an old blanket," James said. "One that Blackie hasn't chewed."

"My mom says they might not be able to cope with all six," Mandy said. "But I *would* like the family to stay together, if they can. Wouldn't you?"

"Yes." James looked thoughtful. "We could help take care of them. We could go there after school and feed them . . . things like that. Your mom could tell us what to do."

"I *know* how to look after kittens," Mandy said. "They need a warm bed and food and they need to be groomed every day. They need toys and . . ."

"We solved the problem," said James.

Mandy looked at him. "Della did say we could go and visit anytime we like. James, you're so smart!"

Katie was walking along the pavement as they arrived at school.

"Did anyone call about the cats?" Mandy asked anxiously.

Katie shook her head sadly. "No. Have you found anybody?"

Mandy glanced at James. It would be better not to say anything until she had asked Della.

"No," Mandy said. "But my grandma's going to ask around, and my mom and dad."

"And my mom and dad," James added.

In class, Mrs. Todd had to remind Mandy several times that gazing out the window would not help her learn her math.

"What's the matter with you, Mandy?" she asked when class was over. "You're not yourself today."

"I'm sorry, Mrs. Todd," Mandy said. "I've got a lot on my mind."

"Yes, well, make sure it's schoolwork that's on your mind tomorrow," Mrs. Todd said. "Otherwise you're going to get behind. We don't want that, do we?"

"No, Mrs. Todd." Mandy hung her head. She knew it would be hard to set her mind to *anything* until she had found a place for the kittens. She just couldn't wait to get home and call Westmoor House.

Katie caught up with Mandy just as she was leaving. "No one wants the kittens," she said. Mandy could see she was almost crying. "I've asked everybody." A tear ran down Katie's cheek. "And my dad says he's going to get rid of them."

"Get rid of them?" Mandy asked in horror. "What does he mean?"

Katie shrugged. "I don't know. He just said if they're not gone by Saturday morning he'll get rid of them."

Mandy put her arm around Katie's shoulders. "Don't cry, Katie," she said. "James and I have got a plan."

"What kind of a plan?" Katie asked.

"I can't tell you yet," Mandy told her. "But I promise I'll let you know about it as soon as I can."

"We need to do something soon." Katie wiped her nose with the back of her hand. "Or it's going to be too late." She began to cry even harder. "It's bad enough having to leave all my friends," she sobbed. "But leaving the kittens, too . . ."

Mandy took a tissue from her bag. She gave it to Katie. The little girl blew her nose loudly.

"I'd better get home or my mom will wonder where I am."

"Try not to worry," Mandy said as they went to get their bikes.

Katie sniffed again. "I'll try. And thank you for helping me so far." She looked sad as she rode off in the direction of the church.

Mandy felt very anxious as she rode home with James. It was all right telling Katie not to worry. But how was she going to stop worrying herself?

"Can't stop," Mandy said as they arrived at James's gate. "I want to call Della as soon as I can."

"Good luck," James said.

"I'll let you know what she says," Mandy called as she rushed off. "Keep your fingers crossed."

"I will!" James shouted.

Mandy skidded to a halt outside her gate and flung it open. She propped her bike up against the wall and hurried in through the waiting room door of Animal Ark.

Mrs. McFarlane from the general store was

sitting on one of the chairs. She had a cage on her lap. Inside it was a green bird with all its feathers fluffed up. It looked very upset about something.

"Oh, dear." Mandy stopped in her tracks. She sat down next to Mrs. McFarlane and peered at the bird. "What's wrong with Sparky?" She put her finger through the bars. Sparky ignored it.

"I don't know," said Mrs. McFarlane. "He's been like this for a couple of days."

"Maybe he's lonely," Mandy suggested. "Perhaps he would like a friend?"

Mandy almost suggested a kitten, then decided that wasn't a good idea. Birds and kittens definitely did not mix!

Mrs. McFarlane sighed. "A friend?"

"Yes," Mandy said. "Birds live in flocks in the wild. Most people only have one, but birds do like having a friend."

"You could be right," Mrs. McFarlane said. "I'll see what your mom says, Mandy. He's been quite content with talking to himself in his mirror up till now."

Mandy stood up. "You don't know anyone who wants a kitten, do you?"

"I've already asked," Jean Knox said as she came in from the back room.

"I'm sorry, Mandy, I don't," Mrs. McFarlane said. "I don't think poor Sparky would take kindly to a kitten."

"No," Mandy said. "Neither do I."

"I'll ask my customers, if you like," Mrs.

McFarlane offered. "Most people come in at some time or another."

"It's got to be soon," Mandy said.

"I'll do my best," Mrs. McFarlane promised.

"Has anyone else seen my ad?" Mandy asked Jean.

"One or two people," Jean said. "That's all, I'm afraid."

"Not to worry," Mandy said. "If I'm lucky, I might find a home for them all this evening."

"Oh?" Jean raised her eyebrows. "All of them?"

"Yes," Mandy said with a grin. "The whole litter!"

Mandy dashed on through into the house. She dumped her bag in the hall and quickly looked up the number of Westmoor House. She dialed the numbers and tapped her fingers on the table.

"Please hurry," she muttered under her breath. "Please . . ."

But when someone did answer, it wasn't Della.

"I'm afraid she's out," the voice said.

"Oh." Mandy's heart sank. Every minute was precious. Every passing hour took the kittens closer and closer to being "gotten rid of."

"When will she be back?" Mandy asked anxiously.

"About seven, I think," the voice told her. "Can I give her a message?"

Mandy thought it would be much better to talk to Della herself. "No," she said quickly. "I'll try later, thank you."

Mandy put down the phone with a sigh. She looked at the clock on the wall. Two and a half hours! How was she going to be able to wait that long?

Mandy was sitting at the kitchen table writing in her journal when Dr. Emily came in from the clinic.

Mandy looked up. "Did you find out what was wrong with Sparky?" she asked.

"He just needed a little rest," Dr. Emily said.

"And you'll be pleased to know Mrs. McFarlane is going to get him a friend."

Mandy smiled. "That's great, Mom."

Dr. Emily went to put the kettle on. "Did you have a good day at school, Mandy?"

"No, terrible," Mandy said. "I've been thinking about Katie's kittens all day."

"Have you called Westmoor House?" her mom asked.

Mandy nodded and told her what had happened.

Dr. Emily came up with a solution. "I know," she said. "I've got to deliver some antibiotics to Syke Farm later. Why don't we stop at Westmoor House on the way?"

Mandy jumped up and gave her mom a hug. It would be *much* better to ask about the kittens in person.

"Oh, Mom, that would be great! Can James come?" She knew James would hate to be left out.

"If his mom says it's okay," Dr. Emily said. "Call and ask, if you like."

James *did* want to come. He was waiting by his gate later when Dr. Emily drove up in the car. She opened the door.

"Hop in," she said.

"Thanks." James climbed into the backseat.

"I can't wait to see Della," Mandy told him excitedly. "Mom thinks therapy cats are a great idea, don't you, Mom?"

Dr. Emily nodded. "Yes, but it's Della you've got to convince, not me."

They arrived at the home just as Della pulled up in her car. She smiled when she saw Mandy.

"Not more cakes?" she said, her blue eyes twinkling.

"No." Mandy laughed. "We've come to ask you a favor."

"Oh?" Della said.

Mandy quickly introduced her mom, then started to explain what they had come for. All her words seemed to come out too quickly.

". . . And you see, we thought the residents would love them, didn't we, James?" she blurted out.

"Yes," James said, looking up at Della.

Della held up her hand. "I think you'd better come inside and start all over again," she said.

When they got inside, Della took Dr. Emily, Mandy, and James into her office.

"Do sit down," she said. "Now, Mandy, your friend Katie has got six unwanted kittens . . . right, now continue."

Mandy finished the story. "And Katie's dad is going to get rid of them," she said desperately. "Tomorrow!"

Della looked thoughtful. "Six cats." She shook her head slowly. "Mandy, it's an awful lot."

"Maybe you could just take two," James said. "Or three . . . or . . ."

"But we would *really* like them all to stay together," Mandy said quickly. "Wouldn't we, James?"

"Yes," James agreed.

Della sat with her hands clasped together.

"It would be horrible for them to be split up," Mandy went on. "You said some of the people in here were sad because they didn't have families. I know they would understand how the kittens feel."

Della got up out of her chair. "Yes, you're right, Mandy. Well, let's go and ask some of the residents. Let's see what *they* think about having some kitten friends!"

6

A Vote

Della took Mandy, James, and Dr. Emily down
a long carpeted corridor. There was a big room
at the end. The buzz of talking and the sound of
a television turned up loud came from inside.

Della opened the door and ushered them in.
The room was full of people doing all sorts of
things.

Four elderly gentlemen sat at a small table playing cards. In one corner several people were watching television. A very old man was asleep in a chair by the wide bay window, and two ladies sat nearby reading newspapers.

Everyone looked up as they came in. Mandy felt suddenly shy as all eyes turned toward her. She reached up and gripped her mom's hand.

Della went across the room and turned down the television.

"Excuse me, everybody," she said in a loud voice. "I've got a young lady here who wants you to hear an idea she has."

Della took Mandy's hand and led her to the center of the room. "Now, Mandy, tell everyone what you've just told me."

Mandy suddenly felt very nervous. Everyone was staring at her. One or two people began to mutter among themselves.

Mandy threw her mom a pleading glance. Dr. Emily nodded encouragingly.

"Go on, Mandy," she said. "This is your big chance."

Her mom was right. This was her big chance. Perhaps it was her *only* chance to save six precious little lives.

She cleared her throat. "Um . . ." she began. "I was watching TV with my grandpa . . ."

"You'll have to speak up, dear." A loud voice came from an old lady in the corner. "Some of us are a bit hard of hearing."

Mandy shuffled her feet. "Sorry," she said.

Then, in a bold voice, Mandy told the story of the kittens. She told everyone how she had heard about therapy dogs from her grandpa.

". . . And I thought," she said when she had almost finished, "that a great big house like this *should* have some pets." She turned around to look at all the people watching her. "And all those empty laps should have a cat on them," she added as an afterthought.

Everyone laughed and clapped their hands.

"Hear, hear," said one of the old gentlemen who had been playing cards. "I used to have a black cat. I still miss him."

"Me, too," said a lady by the television. She

had put down her knitting to listen to Mandy. "I'd love a cat." She turned to her friend, a tiny lady in a floral dress. "How about you, Dora?" she shouted in her ear.

Dora nodded and smiled at Mandy.

"I hate cats," one of the men suddenly piped up. "Noisy and smelly. Got fleas, all of 'em."

Mandy's heart sank. What if other residents felt the same?

"Oh, George." Della went to sit on the arm of the man's chair. "They would be very well-behaved, I'm sure."

The old man screwed up his nose. "Hate 'em," he mumbled.

Suddenly a very old lady sitting with her legs up on a stool spoke loudly. "Well, I adore cats," she said. "So you can be quiet, George."

"Hear, hear," said someone else. "Be quiet, George, why don't you?"

Mandy felt sorry for George. He was only telling everybody how he felt.

Della rose and came over to Mandy. "That's

Mrs. Brown," she explained. "She's the one who's a hundred years old tomorrow."

"Oh," Mandy whispered. She just couldn't imagine what it felt like to have lived for a hundred years.

"Come and meet her."

Della took Mandy and James over to Mrs. Brown. She introduced them and they shook hands.

Mrs. Brown had the palest, most wrinkled face Mandy had ever seen. She gazed at Mandy with kindly pale blue eyes.

"You love animals, don't you, dear?" she asked in a soft, wavering voice.

"Oh, yes," Mandy breathed. "So does James."

"And so do I," Mrs. Brown said. "I've had lots of pets in my time and I really miss them." She gazed up at Della. "Why don't we take a vote on it, Della?"

"Good idea." Della marched back into the center of the room and clapped her hands. Everyone fell silent again. "All those in favor of adopting the kittens raise your hands."

Mandy held her breath. A forest of hands rose into the air. Mandy gave a sigh of relief. It looked as if almost everyone liked the idea.

"Against?" Della said.

Two people put up their hands. One was George, the man who hated cats. Mrs. Brown frowned at him. He put his hand down sharply and began mumbling to himself.

The only other person who objected was a

man whose name was Tom. He had been asleep in the corner and had only woken up halfway through the voting.

"Don't worry about Tom," Della said. "He always objects to everything." She smiled at Mandy and James. "There you are. It looks as if your kittens have found a home."

Mandy clapped her hands together.

"Oh, thank you, Della!" Mandy looked around. "Thank you, everybody!" She ran to hug her mom. "Mom, isn't it great?"

Dr. Emily looked very pleased. "It certainly is, Mandy."

James was so overjoyed, he couldn't speak. He just stood and grinned.

"I know you'll love them," Mandy said to Mrs. Brown.

"Yes, dear. I'm really looking forward to seeing these kittens of yours."

"They're not mine," Mandy said with a chuckle. "They're yours!"

They left the old people talking excitedly. Della went with them to the front door.

"I'm worried about finding the time to look after them," she said.

"They're only six weeks old," Dr. Emily said. "They'll still need a lot of care."

"James and I have got it all worked out," Mandy said. "We'll come up every day after school and help you. Would that be all right?"

"That would be wonderful, Mandy," Della said. "Is that all right with you, Dr. Emily?"

"I don't want you neglecting your school-work, Mandy," Dr. Emily said.

"I won't, honestly. In fact, helping out with the kittens could be *part* of my schoolwork."

"What do you mean?" Della looked puzzled.

Mandy explained about the diary.

"I'll keep a *kitten* journal," she said. "When I've been up to visit them I'll write all about them and how they're doing. I'll make a special copy for the residents."

"What a clever daughter you've got, Dr. Emily," said Della.

Mandy's mom rolled her eyes. "Yes, don't I know it!"

"When will you bring the kittens over?" Della asked.

"Tomorrow, if that's all right," Mandy said.

"I'll look forward to seeing you. Oh, by the way," Della added, "will they need shots of any sort?"

"They'll need shots against cat flu when they're a bit older," Mandy said before Dr. Emily had time to answer. "And they'll need some worm tablets, too, later on."

"Don't worry," Dr. Emily assured Della. "Bring them to the clinic when they're around three months old and I'll see to it."

"Thanks." Della opened the door for them. "I'll make a special place for the kittens by the stove in the kitchen. Thank you, Mandy. I think you've made a lot of people here very happy."

"Thank *you*," Mandy said. "I hope to see you tomorrow!"

"We *are* going to have an exciting day," Della commented. "A birthday party *and* maybe six new residents."

Mandy hummed as they drove back toward

the village. The sun was going down and the sky looked like a red blanket.

Mandy thought about the kittens, curled up with their mother in that damp shed in Katie's garden. Soon they would all have a lovely new home and lots of people to cuddle them.

Mandy knew the residents would love them all. Even George!

By the time they had returned from Syke Farm it was getting dark.

"You can call Katie as soon as we get in," Dr. Emily said as they dropped James off and headed toward Animal Ark. "She'll be very happy, I'm sure."

But when Mandy dialed Katie's number, all she got was a strange tone.

Dr. Adam listened. "That means the phone has been cut off," he said. "It must be because they're moving in the morning. If you go early, you're bound to catch them," he told Mandy. "It takes ages to load those moving vans."

But Mandy's heart started to beat fast. What if they were too late? What if Katie's father had already carried out his threat?

What if he had "gotten rid" of the kittens before Mandy and James could pick them up?

Mandy thought tomorrow couldn't come soon enough.

7

Six Missing Kittens

"We're too late. They must have left early!"

Mandy's hand flew to her mouth as she and James ran down the front path of Katie's house the following morning.

The house was all boarded up, silent and empty. The family had left.

Blackie pulled excitedly at his leash. Even an empty house was an adventure to him.

Mandy banged on the front door. The sound echoed down the deserted hall. Mandy's heart pounded. There was no one there. Now what were they going to do?

A man came out of the house next door.

"They're gone," he told Mandy and James. "Loaded the van last night and left about an hour ago."

"Did they take the kittens?" Mandy asked anxiously.

"Kittens?" the man said. Then he shrugged. "I don't know anything about any kittens."

"Let's go and look in the shed," James said. They pushed open the side gate and ran round the path. The shed door was open.

James peered inside. "It's no good," he said. "They're not here. I wonder what they've done with them?"

Mandy sat down on the back step and burst into tears. "I don't know," she sobbed. She couldn't bear to think what might have happened to the kittens. "And what are we going to tell Della? The residents will be so upset."

James sat beside her, looking sad. Blackie had gone into the shed. They could hear him scrabbling about. Then he came out with a piece of old blanket in his mouth.

James grabbed it. "Let go!" he commanded. Blackie growled. He hung on more tightly than ever. He shook the piece of rag as if it were a rat.

"Blackie!" James said sternly.

At last Blackie let it go.

"It's the kittens' blanket," Mandy said, crying even harder.

"Maybe they've taken them with Tabby after all!" James tried to cheer Mandy up. "Because they couldn't find homes."

Mandy shook her head. "No. Katie said her dad was going to get rid of them. But where, that's what I'd like to know."

Blackie came to lick the tears off Mandy's cheeks. She buried her face in his soft fur.

After a while Mandy stopped crying. She stood up and squared her shoulders. Crying wouldn't bring the kittens back. She and James would just have to go and explain to Della what had happened.

"We'd better go and tell my mom first," Mandy sniffed. "She was going to examine the kittens before we took them to Westmoor House. She'll be wondering where we've gone to."

Mandy and James made their way back to Animal Ark.

The postman, Bill Ward, had just pulled up in his van outside the newsstand. He stopped there every morning to get his daily newspaper.

"You two look very sad," he said when he saw Mandy and James. "What's up?"

"We've lost six kittens," James said.

"Six kittens?" Mr. Ward looked surprised. "How on earth can you lose six kittens?"

Mandy explained.

"That's funny," Mr. Ward said. "I passed John Greene's car this morning. It was right up the

moorland road. I wondered what he was doing up there at the crack of dawn. Where were they moving to, do you know?"

Mandy shook her head. "No. It was far away because Katie has to go to a new school. Was there a moving van with them?"

"No, I just saw his car heading for the moors." Bill shook his head. "Seems a bit odd to go for a drive the day you're moving to a new house." He shrugged. "Oh, well, people are strange sometimes."

He said good-bye to Mandy and James and drove off.

Mandy watched him go with a frown on her face. She knew that narrow moorland road. It led right up to High Tor. She had been up there a few times with her mom and dad. They hadn't been going for a drive, though. They had been going up there for a special reason.

She turned to James. "Quick!" she gasped. "I bet I know where Mr. Greene was going."

"Where?" James called as Mandy hurried on ahead. He dashed after her, Blackie pulling at the leash.

Mandy had already reached her house. Dr. Adam was in the driveway, cleaning the mud off his car.

"Dad!" Mandy said breathlessly. "Are you busy?"

"Not really," Dr. Adam said. "I'm off duty this morning."

"Could you take us up to the Welford Animal Shelter, please?"

Dr. Adam frowned. "What on earth for? I thought you were supposed to be picking up those kittens."

"We are," Mandy said. "But when we got to Katie's house, everyone was gone."

"Gone? What about the kittens?"

"I've got a feeling Mr. Greene might have taken them up to the shelter. Please, Dad," Mandy urged. "Can we go and see?"

Dr. Adam opened the car door. "We certainly can," he said. "Hop in, you two."

Mandy's heart pounded as Dr. Adam drove through the village. He headed up the moorland road toward the Welford Animal Shelter. The shelter was run by a woman named Betty Hilder. She took in all kinds of unwanted and abandoned animals. It would be just the place to take the kittens.

When they reached the shelter, a donkey in the field next to Betty's bungalow brayed a greeting. The sound of dogs barking came from the row of kennels behind the house.

Mandy ran up the path and rang the doorbell.

"I'm here," a voice called from one of the barns.

Betty came out to greet them. "Hello, Mandy, what brings you here?"

Dr. Adam and James got out of the car. They all began talking at once.

"Well," she said when they had finished, "as a matter of fact . . ." She paused in mid-sentence. "Better still, come and see for yourselves."

Betty led them around to the back door. She opened it and they followed her inside. She took them through to the kitchen. In front of the stove was a cardboard box.

"There," Betty said. "Are they what you're looking for?"

Mandy ran across the room and kneeled down. There, all curled up and sleepy, were the six tiny kittens.

Mandy let out a sob of relief. "James, Dad, it's them! Oh, thank goodness!"

James ran and kneeled beside her. "It's them, all right," he said to Dr. Adam. "Come and see."

Dr. Adam took out one of the kittens. It

made a soft mewing noise. Dr. Adam frowned. "This one's a bit thin," he said.

Betty came to kneel beside them. "Yes, they all are. I found them on the doorstep when I got up this morning. They've had some warm milk already but they'd probably like some more." She went to heat some milk on the stove.

Dr. Adam was examining the other kittens.

"They are all right, aren't they, Dad?" Mandy asked anxiously. "I had a feeling they weren't being looked after very well."

Her dad nodded. "They need to put on a bit of weight. They're all healthy enough, but they're going to need special care for a few days."

"Oh, no," Mandy said, her heart sinking. "Della's very busy with the party and everything."

"Della?" Betty came back with the milk. She poured it into three saucers.

Mandy and James placed the kittens, two by two, in front of them. They began lapping up the milk. Their tiny tongues flicked in and out so fast they were just a blur.

Mandy explained about Westmoor House.

"How wonderful," Betty said. "I'm so pleased the kittens are going to stay together. They're such a sweet little family."

"But I don't know how Della's going to find time to give them special care." Mandy sounded worried.

"I'd look after them myself," said Betty, "but we've got a full house at the moment."

Dr. Adam was stroking his beard thought-fully. "Maybe we could have them at Animal Ark for a while," he said.

Mandy drew in her breath. Six kittens at the clinic! Six kittens for her to look after. It would be like a dream come true.

"Oh, Dad!" she cried. "Could we really?"

Dr. Adam winked at Betty. "Oh, I should think so," he said. "Just this once."

Mandy felt like cheering. This had to be one of the best days of her life.

8

Blackie Solves a Problem

A day or so later, the kittens were well and settled at Animal Ark.

As a special treat, Dr. Adam and Dr. Emily let Mandy keep them up in her bedroom. They had a brand-new wooden box that Grandpa had made, and James's mom had sent over a special blanket. The box stood against the warm radiator.

Dr. Emily found six little dishes for their milk. Mandy insisted they each have one of their own — and Dr. Adam had found a litter tray for them to use while they were there.

Mandy gave all the kittens names. She wrote the names down in her kitten journal.

She called the largest black kitten "Pepper."

"Black with a tiny orange tip to her tail," Mandy wrote.

She studied the others. "Sam," she said suddenly. "That's a good name, too." She wrote that down. "All black," she put down, "with a tiny orange spot over one eye."

She went on gazing at the kittens. They were rolling around on her bedside rug pretending to fight. They looked full of health. Their eyes were bright and their tummies were quite chubby now and full of milk.

"Pumpkin," she said. "That sounds pretty good." She wrote it down. Then "Carrots" because the color of the kitten's fur reminded Mandy of the orange carrots Grandpa grew in his vegetable garden.

Mandy thought about the residents of the home. She felt sure they would like the name "Carrots," too.

There were two kittens left. Both were black *and* orange. The smaller of the two was very lively. He had already managed to climb up Mandy's quilt and onto her bed.

"I know," Mandy said suddenly. "Clown . . . that's a good name for a naughty boy like you.

And . . ." Then she remembered the old man at the home who said he didn't like cats. "George," Mandy decided. She wrote it down, then looked at the page filled with names. "He's bound to like you if you're named after him."

Mandy went to pick up George. She gave him a cuddle and rubbed his soft fur against her cheek.

"There you are," she said, feeling satisfied. "Now you've all got names. I can't wait to introduce you to your new owners."

Mandy felt a pang of sadness. She would really miss the kittens. Having them here was like having her very own pets. Then she smiled to herself. Six kittens were a handful. They needed much more space than her small bedroom. Della would still need help, so that meant Mandy would still see a lot of the kittens and they would always be very special to her.

A few days after that, Dr. Adam declared the kittens fit to go to their new home.

"We'll take them on Saturday morning," he told Mandy.

Mandy had been very busy looking after the kittens. She fed them and cleaned out their tray every morning before she went to school. She rushed home after school to feed them again. Then she played with them before dinner. Because they no longer had their mother to groom them, Mandy did it instead. She found a little soft brush and groomed their fur.

Each day Mandy checked their ears to make sure they were clean. Then she bathed their eyes gently with cotton.

Last thing every night, Mandy wrote in her journal. There were lots of things for her to write about. In fact, the journal was almost full.

In the journal were the names and details of all the kittens. Mandy had written down what they liked to eat and what games they liked to play. She also wrote what happened each day.

On the day before the kittens were ready to go to their new home, Mandy made her last entry.

It had been six days since Mr. Greene had left the kittens at Betty's shelter.

Mandy wrote:

<u>Kitten Day 6</u>
The last day at Animal Ark.
Morning: I gave Pepper, Carrots, Pumpkin, George, Clown, and Sam their breakfast. Pepper stole some of Pumpkin's. George stole some of Sam's. Clown pushed his bowl under the chair and ate his there. He doesn't like the other kittens watching him eat his breakfast.
Evening: I gave the kittens a special bath and brushed them. They start their new jobs as therapy cats tomorrow at Westmoor House. George was naughty. He ran under my dressing table and would not come out. Clown climbed on my bed and got lost under the quilt. James came and almost sat on top of him. The others were good. I know I'll feel sad when the kittens have gone.

Mandy made a special copy of the journal for Della and the residents.

She hoped her journal would be one of the most interesting ones in the class. After all, who else would have had six kittens to write about?

On Saturday morning, Dr. Emily came upstairs to Mandy's bedroom. She was carrying a big basket with a wire door on the front. It was a special basket for carrying cats and kittens.

All the kittens were asleep in their box. Mandy felt very proud as she gently took them out, one by one. They were all sleek and healthy. They yawned and stretched, then sat up and began washing themselves. It was as if they knew they were going somewhere special.

Mandy took their blanket from the box and put it in the basket. She knew they would like to have their own blanket in their new home.

She put the kittens inside the basket. All except Clown. He had disappeared, as usual.

Mandy lay on her stomach and looked under

the bed. Clown was there, playing with a pencil that Mandy had dropped.

Mandy stretched out her arm and picked him up. "Oh, you!" she said. She kissed his tiny nose. Then she carefully put him into the basket and closed the wire door.

Mandy picked up the basket and took it downstairs. Dr. Emily followed with the wooden box.

Dr. Adam was in the kitchen getting ready to go out on a call. "Ready?" he asked.

"Yep," Mandy said. She couldn't hide the sadness in her voice. "You'd better say goodbye to our kitten crowd."

Dr. Adam peered into the basket. "Well, Mandy," he said. "They look terrific. You've certainly done a good job of looking after them."

"Thanks, Dad." Mandy sighed. "I'm really going to miss them."

Dr. Adam gave her a hug. "I'm sure you'll still see lots of them."

Mandy managed a smile. "Yes, I know, but it won't be the same as having them here."

Dr. Emily gave Mandy her car keys. "You'd better put the kittens in the back of the car," she said. "I've just got to check my appointments. I'll bring their box out with me."

As Mandy went out the front door with the basket, James came walking along the road with Blackie. They were going to come with Mandy and Dr. Emily to deliver the kittens.

"Hi, James." Mandy put the basket down on the sidewalk. She gave Blackie a hug. Blackie sniffed at the basket, his tail wagging. He would have loved to play with the kittens.

"Have you finished your journal?" James asked Mandy when he had said hello to the kittens.

Mandy suddenly realized she had left Della's copy upstairs in her room.

"Yep," she said. "But I forgot to bring it down. I'll be right back."

Mandy rushed back inside.

Dr. Adam was just leaving. "What's up?"

"I forgot my journal," Mandy said as she rushed past him. She ran up the stairs. Blackie jerked away from James and followed her up.

"Hey!" James scooted inside after him.

Blackie was running up the staircase. The Labrador dived into Mandy's room and grabbed her old teddy bear from the chair. He began shaking it, ready for a game.

"Blackie!" Mandy was just getting the journal from her desk. James arrived, looking red in the face.

"Sorry," he gasped.

Blackie ran out and raced along the landing. Shouting, Mandy ran after him. "Drop it!"

she commanded when she caught him halfway through the bathroom door.

Blackie wagged his tail.

Mandy frowned and tried to sound angry. "Drop it!" she said again.

Blackie suddenly dropped the teddy at her feet. She rubbed his head. "Good boy!"

"Good boy!" James gasped. "When has Blackie ever been good?"

"You must give him lots of praise," Mandy said in a knowing voice.

"What, even when he steals your things?" James said.

"No, when he gives them back." Mandy laughed. "Come on, my mom will wonder what's happened."

When they got back downstairs, Dr. Emily was still in the clinic. Mandy went to put the basket into the back of the car. It was then that she saw the door of the basket had swung open.

The kittens were nowhere to be seen!

"Oh, James!" Mandy gasped in horror. She

spun around. How could six kittens disappear in such a short time? Now what were they going to do?

Blackie was sniffing at the blanket. Then, nose to the ground, he headed off into the shrubbery.

"Quick!" James ran after him. "I bet he can smell them."

Mandy followed. They could hear Blackie snuffling around under one of the bushes.

Mandy bent down. There, playing with some dead leaves, were two of the kittens. She heaved a sigh of relief. She couldn't think *what* she would have done if they were lost forever.

"Good boy!" she said to Blackie. She reached out and picked up the kittens, Pepper and Pumpkin. "I've got two, James," she called.

Mandy put the kittens in the basket and shut the door firmly.

James had run down the path. "Here's George," he called, scooping the kitten up into his arms. He suddenly dived to one side. "And here's Sam." Sam was sitting at the bottom of the tall tree by the gate. He had been playing with a feather he had found on the path. James scooped him up, too, and returned them both to the basket.

Mandy was looking around. "Thank goodness," she said. "Now . . . two more. Carrots and Clown. Oh, James, where have they gone?"

Blackie had run around the side of the house. Suddenly they heard a thud hitting the ground. Mandy and James looked at each other, then ran after Blackie. If anyone could find the two missing kittens, it was Blackie.

But Blackie was standing with his paws on the garbage can. He had reached up and knocked off the plastic lid with his nose. It was one of his favorite tricks.

Mandy grabbed his collar. "The kittens won't be in there, silly," she said. She pushed Blackie forward. "Find them, please, Blackie."

Just then she heard a small meow. She spun around, frowning. Where was it coming from?

James ran to look in the shed. The door was shut tight so he came back to Mandy.

"They won't be in there. . . ." he began.

Mandy held her finger to her lips. "Shh."

Mandy heard the kitten again. The sound seemed to be coming from somewhere near her feet.

Then the garbage can lid began to move. Mandy jumped back in surprise. James stared at it, wide-eyed. The lid moved again. Blackie gave a little yelp and crept away, his tail between his legs.

Then Mandy gave a shout. She knew exactly what was making the lid move. She picked it up. There, underneath, looking dazed, crouched Carrots. The lid must have fallen on top of him when Blackie knocked it off.

"Poor old Carrots," James said.

Mandy picked up the kitten and hugged him to her. She quickly felt his back and legs. "He's okay," she said. "Blackie, you're the cleverest dog in the world." Blackie was sitting by the hedge, looking sorry for himself.

"And the naughtiest." James gave his dog a hug. Blackie wriggled out of his grasp and ran to the front gate.

They quickly searched the back garden but there was no sign of the last kitten. They hurried back to the basket and put Carrots inside.

Dr. Emily came out of the clinic with the kittens' box.

"Sorry I've been so long," she said. "I had to take a telephone call. Come on, let's get going."

Mandy quickly explained what had happened.

"Clown's still missing," she said. "We can't go until we've found him."

"He can't have gone far." Dr. Emily looked around. "Maybe he went back indoors?"

Mandy shook her head. "He couldn't have. The door's been shut all the time."

James had followed Blackie back to the bottom of the tree. Blackie looked up and suddenly began barking.

"Over here!" James shouted.

James was looking up into the branches. He pointed. "Up there," he said.

Mandy gasped. She suddenly felt wobbly at the knees. There, sitting on one of the highest branches, was Clown, the naughtiest kitten of them all!

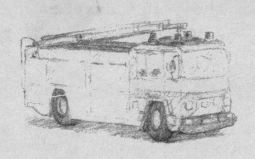

9

The Best Presents

"Well, well, what *have* we got here?"

Mandy turned to see Mrs. McFarlane standing behind her. She was gazing up into the tree.

"A kitten," Mandy told her. "Stuck."

"Better call the fire department," Mrs. McFarlane said. "You'll never get him down on your own."

"I think we should try first," Dr. Emily said. She went around the back to get a ladder. But when she put it up against the tree it only reached halfway.

By now, other people from the village had arrived. Walter Pickard had been on his way to the shop. He stood gazing up into the tree, shaking his head.

"My, my," he said. "That *is* a long way up."

Then Grandpa arrived on his bike.

"What's going on, Emily?" he asked.

When she told him, he burst out laughing. "Mandy Hope," he said. "What will you do next?"

"It's not funny, Grandpa," Mandy said, close to tears.

Grandpa stood with his chin in his hand. "Maybe you could persuade him to climb down."

Mandy shook her head. "He's too scared."

Mandy's teacher, Mrs. Todd, drove up in her car. She got out to see what all the commotion was about.

"Well, Mandy," she said when Dr. Emily explained what was happening. "This is going to be something to put in your journal."

Mandy was growing more and more anxious. Everyone was talking about Clown, but no one was *doing* anything.

"I think we *had* better get the fire department," Dr. Emily said at last. "I'll explain to them on the phone." She disappeared indoors.

Mandy stood gazing up at Clown. He was crouched on a fragile branch looking very

frightened. She didn't think she could bear it if he made a sudden movement and fell off. "Please, please stay still, Clown," she whispered. "We'll get you down, I know we will."

James was crouched down, his face buried in Blackie's neck. It seemed he couldn't bear to look, either.

It wasn't long before the fire engine came roaring along the village street toward them. It pulled up outside Animal Ark.

Six burly firefighters piled out.

"All right," the chief said. "Where's this kitten?"

Mandy pointed. "Up there," she said anxiously. "He's very scared. Please, can you get him down?"

The chief tipped his helmet back on his head. He gazed upward. Then he made a salute. "Don't you worry, young lady," he said. "We'll do our best."

The firefighters got their long ladder from the top of the engine. With a screech and a clang they put it up against the tree. Higher and higher it went, until it almost reached the branch where Clown was crouched. One of the firefighters began to climb. When he got to the top he stretched out his arms.

Mandy held her breath. The firefighter's fingers were inches away from Clown. The kitten gave a small meow and moved backward.

By now, quite a crowd had gathered. Everyone gave a gasp.

Then the firefighter shook his head and began to climb back down.

"I'm sorry," he said when he reached the bottom. "That branch is too fragile to hold my weight. I'm not sure we're going to be able to get him."

Everyone began talking among themselves.

"We'll have to call for a longer ladder," the chief was saying.

Mandy stared up at Clown. It could be a long time before another ladder arrived. She had to *do* something. If the branch wouldn't hold the firefighter's weight, maybe it would hold hers.

Mandy looked at James and held her finger

to her lips. His mouth fell open when he saw what Mandy intended to do. James began to shake his head. "Mandy, no!" he hissed.

Blackie lay down and hid his face in his paws.

But Mandy had made up her mind. She was going to rescue Clown herself.

She began to climb the ladder. Up and up until she felt she might almost touch the sky. She didn't dare look down. Right at the top she stepped carefully onto Clown's branch.

"Now don't move," she told him sternly. "Stay where you are and I can reach you."

Mandy clung on tight. Her heart was thudding like a drum. She crawled slowly along the branch toward the kitten. Then she stretched out her hand and scooped him up. The kitten clung to her, glad to be rescued at last.

Below, Mandy heard Dr. Emily shout, "Mandy, what are you doing!" She had been talking to Grandpa with her back to the ladder and had only just noticed what Mandy was up to.

But Mandy was already on her way down. When she reached the bottom, everyone cheered.

Dr. Emily grabbed her arm. "Mandy, you shouldn't have done that. You might have fallen!" She looked angry.

Mandy hung her head. Now that she was back down, she realized just how dangerous her climb had been. "I'm sorry, Mom. I couldn't leave poor little Clown up there any longer."

Dr. Emily put her arm around Mandy and gave her a hug.

"Don't you ever do anything like that again," she said.

Soon Clown was tucked safely back in with the other kittens.

Mandy thanked the firefighters. She watched as the fire engine roared off down the main street. It wasn't every day that there was an exciting rescue in the sleepy village.

★　　★　　★

When the kitten basket was safely in the back of the car they set off for Westmoor House.

"You'd better leave Blackie in the car," Dr. Emily told James when they arrived at Westmoor House. "He'll only cause havoc. We've had enough trouble for one day!"

"Okay." James rolled down the window a little so that Blackie had some fresh air.

One of Della's helpers opened the door. "Come in, come in," he said. "Everyone's waiting."

Mandy felt excited as they marched along the hall toward the big living room at the end. She and James carried the basket between them. With six chubby kittens inside, it was quite heavy.

In the living room everyone stopped talking and turned to look at them. One man went to turn off the television.

"Hurrah!" someone called. "They're here!"

Mandy smiled and nodded. Della rose from a chair by the fire and came over.

"We've all been so excited," she said. She

peered into the basket, then drew in her breath. "Oh, they're so sweet! Look, everyone!"

Mandy put down the basket. She opened the door a little and took out one of the kittens.

"This is Sam." She took him over and gave him to a lady sitting by the window.

Then she took out another one. "This is Carrots," she announced.

Everyone smiled and laughed. "What a good name," one of the men called. He held out his arms. "Can I hold him?"

James took Carrots and placed him in the old man's arms.

"I've got a cat, too," James whispered.

"What's his name?" the old gentleman asked.

"Benji," said James. "He's big and fluffy. I've got a puppy as well. He's named Blackie."

"I used to have a dog," the old man told him. "But a cat will do just as well." He smiled down at Carrots. The kitten was purring and rubbing his face against the old man's woolly cardigan.

"This is Pepper." Mandy bent down to take the black kitten from the basket.

Pepper wriggled and jumped out of her arms. She scampered over to Mrs. Brown and began to climb up the leg of her stool. Della went to rescue her. She put her on Mrs. Brown's lap. Pepper curled up and began to purr gently. The old lady's face lit up as she stroked the kitten's soft fur.

"Thank you, Mandy," she said. "Pepper is going to be my favorite."

"And this is Clown." Mandy lifted the kitten out. Clown seemed no different after his ordeal in the tree. "He's *really* bad," Mandy said. She looked around. "Who wants him?"

A dozen arms were outstretched. "Give him to Tom," Della suggested.

Mandy took the kitten over to Tom. Tom was sitting with his back to everyone. Mandy tapped him gently on the shoulder. "Would you like to hold this one?" she said softly.

Tom mumbled something that Mandy could not hear.

"Please," she said. "You'll feel much better. He'll make you laugh, honestly."

The old man turned slowly. The frown fell from his face when he saw the pretty kitten.

Mandy put Clown gently into Tom's lap. Tom turned away again and softly stroked Clown's head. Mandy could see that Clown was going to be Tom's best friend. She smiled to herself and went back to the basket.

There were two kittens left.

"This is Pumpkin," she said, taking her out. Pumpkin was the laziest of all the kittens. She opened one sleepy eye and yawned.

"I'll have her," said Dora.

Dr. Emily took Pumpkin over. The kitten took one look at Dora, then curled around on her lap and fell fast asleep. Dora smiled. She lay back in her chair and closed her eyes, too.

"Now . . ." Mandy took George out. She went over to the old man who didn't like cats. "He's named after you, George," she said, gazing at the old man.

The old man shook his head and turned away. "Smells!" he said.

"No, he doesn't," Mandy said. "He's clean and beautiful. Look at him."

The old man looked at Mandy. Then he looked at the kitten. He shrugged his shoulders. "If no one else wants him . . ."

"I do," a voice came from the corner. "I'll have the little fellow."

George snatched the kitten from Mandy's arms. "No, you won't," he said. "He's mine!"

"Oh, dear," Dr. Emily said. "I hope they're not going to fight over them."

Della laughed. "I'm sure they'll sort it out." She turned to Mandy and James. "They're beautiful. Thank you so much, you two."

Mandy took her journal from her pocket. She gave it to Della. "This is for you," she said shyly.

Della opened the journal. As well as writing all about them, Mandy had drawn a little picture of each of the cats.

Della drew in her breath.

"It's lovely, Mandy." She took the journal across to Mrs. Brown. "Look at this!"

Soon the journal was being passed around. There were "oohs" and "ahhs" from everyone.

"Did you have a nice party?" Mandy asked Mrs. Brown.

"Yes, thank you, dear. It was lovely," the old lady told her.

"Did you get lots of presents?"

"Quite a few," Mrs. Brown said. "But these kittens are the best present of all."

Dr. Emily looked at her watch. "I'm afraid we've got to go. I've got some calls to make."

"We'll come up tomorrow and help feed them," Mandy said as they made their way to the front door.

"That would be very nice, Mandy," Della said. "Although I've got a feeling there're going to be plenty of willing hands to look after our new family. You've made a lot of people very happy."

"No," Mandy said. "It's the *kittens* who are going to make them happy!"

On the way home, James sat in the backseat with Blackie. "Do you think they'd like a therapy puppy, too?" he joked, struggling to stop the puppy from chewing the seat belt.

Dr. Emily chuckled. "Not one like Blackie, I don't think. They would never cope!"

10

The Winner

At school the following Monday, everyone was talking about their journals and the things they had put in them.

"I didn't have anything exciting to write," one of the boys said. "All I did was go to school, eat my dinner, and watch television."

"I went to my aunt's," someone else said.

"My brother broke his leg playing football," a friend of Mandy's told her. "So I wrote all about that."

"I went to Walton and got a new pair of shoes," another friend said.

"I went on a train through the Channel Tunnel," someone said. "It was great."

At last the time came for the class to read their journals. Mandy realized she had so much to cram into hers that it might take the whole class to read out loud.

When Mandy's turn came, she stood up and cleared her throat.

"Kitten Journal," she said in a loud voice. For some reason she didn't feel nervous anymore. "One week in the life of six kittens.

"Kitten Day 1..."

When she had finished, there was silence for a minute. Then everyone clapped.

Mandy blushed and sat down quickly.

"Very good, Mandy," Mrs. Todd said. She looked at a boy named Paul Jackson. "Now, Paul, your turn."

When everyone had read their journal, Mrs. Todd said, "Excellent, everyone. Now, I want you all to write down on a piece of paper whose journal you thought was the best."

Mrs. Todd waited a few minutes, then went around collecting the votes. She sat at her desk counting. Then she looked up. She had a broad smile on her face.

"The winner is . . . Mandy Hope. Very nice, Mandy!"

Mandy turned red as everyone clapped again.

Mrs. Todd opened her desk and took out a bag. "Come and get your first prize, Mandy."

After school Mandy rushed out to show James her prize. It was a book about animals of the rain forests.

"Oooh!" James turned to a picture of a tiger. "I wouldn't like to have to look after one of those."

"I would," Mandy said, jumping on her bike. "I'd love it!"

A warm breeze was blowing as Mandy and James raced across the green. The houses and shops glowed in the afternoon sunshine.

Mandy said good-bye to James at his gate and headed off toward Animal Ark.

She felt sad as she wheeled her bike up the brick path. There wouldn't be any kittens waiting for her today. Mandy knew she would miss them. Then her heart lifted. She would be able to go to Westmoor House to see the kittens whenever she wanted. She knew they would be well looked after and, after all, she did know lots of pets that were *almost* her own.

Mandy pushed open the door of Animal Ark and went inside.

An envelope lay on the kitchen table. It was addressed to Mandy. When she opened it, she saw it was a card from everyone at Westmoor House.

"Thank you for our kittens, Mandy," it said. "They are all wonderful. Come and see us again soon."

Mandy sat back in the chair. She smiled to herself. There was no doubt about it. Finding such a loving home for a whole crowd of kittens had been one of the best things she had ever done.